A Birthday Party for JESUS

God Gave us CHRISTMAS to Celebrate HIS BIRTH

by Susan Jones

Illustrated by Lee Holland

Good Books

New York, New York

There's a quiet flutter
all through the air.
Is it snowflakes? Is it rain?

It's an
INVITATION!

"Is it a
CHRISTMAS
party?"

"It's Jesus's birthday,
my little Bunny,"
said Mama.

Little Bunny was soon
snug in his bed.

He dreamt about all the birthday toys and treats he wanted when it was his birthday.

The next day he came
upon all the animals
decorating the forest.

He hopped here and he hopped there, asking all the other animals, "Does Jesus want toys, like me?!"

"Does he want candy,
like me?! Or games?"
asked Little Bunny.

"No, no. None of those things," answered the Hedgehog.
Little Bunny didn't understand.

Bunny watched as his friends gathered together with their special presents all picked out.

He looked around, and what did he see?

All his friends celebrating Jesus underneath the tree!

He wanted to join them, but he still didn't know what gift to bring!

"But what does he WANT
for his birthday?!"
Little Bunny insisted.

"Take a look over here, my friend," said Badger.

Little Bunny looked closer at all the gifts and was surprised to see that they had words written on their tags.

Were these wishes the animals' presents?

Faith

Charity

Mercy.

Friendship

Kindness

Mercy.

Honesty.

"Can I make one, too?"
asked Little Bunny.

"I know just what he'd like.
And I think I'd like it, too,"
said Little Bunny, grabbing
a box and a marker.

"This is what I want to give Jesus for Christmas! Do you think he'll like it?"

Love

"Yes, Little Bunny," said Mama. "Love is the greatest gift anyone can give on Christmas.

We love Jesus because he loved us first. Love is the whole reason Jesus was born!"

Little Bunny understood. Jesus's birthday is about a love so great it overflows to everyone around you.

His heart full, Little Bunny whispered, "Happy birthday, Jesus!"

Good Books books may be purchased in bulk at special discounts for sales promotion, corporate gifts, fund-raising, or educational purposes. Special editions can also be created to specifications. For details, contact the Special Sales Department, Good Books, 307 West 36th Street, 11th Floor, New York, NY 10018 or info@skyhorsepublishing.com.

Good Books is an imprint of Skyhorse Publishing, Inc.®, a Delaware corporation.

Visit our website at www.goodbooks.com.

10 9 8 7 6 5 4 3

Library of Congress Cataloging-in-Publication Data is available on file.

Cover design by Katie Jennings
Cover illustration by Lee Holland

Print ISBN: 978-1-68099-319-6
Ebook ISBN: 978-1-68099-325-7

Printed in Canada